ABOUT THE BANK STREET READY-TO-READ SERIES

Seventy years of educational research and innovative teaching have given the Bank Street College of Education the reputation as America's most trusted name in early childhood education.

Because no two children are exactly alike in their development, we have designed the *Bank Street Ready-to-Read* series in three levels to accommodate the individual stages of reading readiness of children ages four through eight.

- ○ *Level 1:* GETTING READY TO READ—read-alouds for children who are taking their first steps toward reading.
- ● *Level 2:* READING TOGETHER—for children who are just beginning to read by themselves but may need a little help.
- ○ *Level 3:* I CAN READ IT MYSELF—for children who can read independently.

Our three levels make it easy to select the books most appropriate for a child's development and enable him or her to grow with the series step by step. The *Bank Street Ready-to-Read* books also overlap and reinforce each other, further encouraging the reading process.

We feel that making reading fun and enjoyable is the single most important thing that you can do to help children become good readers. And we hope you'll be a part of Bank Street's long tradition of learning through sharing.

The Bank Street College of Education

To Ariel and Justin
— J.O.

To Ann Stillman
— C.D.

THE DONKEY'S TALE
A Bantam Little Rooster Book
Simultaneous paper-over-board and trade paper editions / June 1991

Little Rooster is a trademark of Bantam Books,
a division of Bantam Doubleday Dell Publishing Group, Inc.

Series graphic design by Alex Jay/Studio J
Associate Editor: Gillian Bucky

Special thanks to James A. Levine, Betsy Gould,
Erin B. Gathrid, and Whit Stillman.

Library of Congress Cataloging-in-Publication Data

Oppenheim, Joanne.
The donkey's tale / by Joanne Oppenheim:
illustrated by Chris Demarest.

p.   cm.—(Bank Street ready-to-read)
''A Byron Preiss book.''
''A Bantam little rooster book.''
Summary: A rhymed retelling of the traditional
fable about the poor man and his son who, on their
way to market to sell their donkey, try to take
the advice of everyone they meet.
ISBN 0-553-07090-8.—ISBN 0-553-35208-3 (pbk.)
[1. Stories in rhyme. 2. Fables.]
I. Demarest, Chris L., ill. II. Title. III. Series.
PZ8.3.0615Tw   1991
[E]—dc20

90-31812   CIP   AC

Published simultaneously in the United States and Canada

Bantam Books are published by Bantam Books, a division of Bantam Doubleday
Dell Publishing Group, Inc. Its trademark, consisting of the words ''Bantam Books''
and the portrayal of a rooster, is Registered in U.S. Patent and Trademark Office
and in other countries. Marca Registrada. Bantam Books, 666 Fifth Avenue, New
York, New York 10103.

PRINTED IN THE UNITED STATES OF AMERICA

0 9 8 7 6 5 4 3 2 1

Bank Street Ready-to-Read™

The Donkey's Tale

by Joanne Oppenheim
Illustrated by Chris Demarest

A Byron Preiss Book

A BANTAM LITTLE ROOSTER BOOK
NEW YORK · TORONTO · LONDON · SYDNEY · AUCKLAND

There once was a farmer
who was poor and old.
He said to his son,
"Our donkey must be sold."

Clip-clop, clip-clop,
they went on their way.
Clip-clop, clip-clop,
on that very hot day.

They had not gone far
down the hot, dusty road,
when they met a man
with a big, heavy load.

"My, my!" said the man,
"What fools you must be.
If I had a donkey,
I'd have the donkey carry me!"

"He's right," said the farmer.
"What he says is true.
Climb on, my son.
Let the donkey carry you!"

Clip-clop, clip-clop,
they went on their way.
Clip-clop, clip-clop,
on that very hot day.

They had not gone far
when whom did they meet?
But a weary old woman
who was resting her feet.

"Shame. Shame on you!"
the old woman cried.
"A young boy should walk!
Your father should ride."

"She's right," said the boy.
"What she says is true.
Come, Father, I'll walk.
Let the donkey carry you!"

Clip-clop, clip-clop,
they went on their way.
Clip-clop, clip-clop,
on that very hot day.

They had not gone far
when whom did they see?
But a man and his wife,
picking apples from a tree.

"Old man!" called the wife.
"How selfish of you!
That donkey could carry
your son and you, too."

"She's right," said the farmer.
"What she says is true.
Both of us can ride—
there's room here for two."

Clip-clop, clip-clop,
they went on their way.
Clip-clop, clip-clop,
on that very hot day.

They had not gone far
when a rider trotted by.
"Fools!" yelled the rider.
"Do you want that beast to die?

Look at that poor donkey.
He's about to fall down!
Why don't the two of you
carry *him* to town?''

"He's right," said the farmer.
"Let's do what he said.
I'll take the back end.
And you take the head!"

With a grunt and a groan
they went on their way.
With a grunt and a groan
on that very hot day.

When they reached the town,
whom should they meet?
But a girl with a gaggle
of geese on the street.

"Carrying a donkey?"
she asked with a giggle.
"Hee-haw!" cried the donkey,
who started to wiggle.

Suddenly the donkey
kicked himself free.
"Hee-haw," he laughed.
"You'll never catch me!"

So the farmer and his son
shouted, "Stop, donkey, stop!"
But the donkey ran away—
clip-clippity-clop.

"Now we've lost our donkey,"
the farmer said with a sigh.
"But why?" asked his son
as he started to cry.

When you try to please everyone,
remember this rule:

You'll end up pleasing no one
and make yourself a fool!